ZZZ

For the children of
Hargrave Park School
F.S.

For Melanie
R.C.

Text copyright © Francesca Simon 1998
Illustrations copyright © Ross Collins 1998

The right of Francesca Simon and Ross Collins to be identified as the author
and illustrator of the Work has been asserted by them in accordance with the Copyright,
Designs and Patents Act 1988.

Published 1998 by Hodder Children's Books
A division of Hodder Headline plc
London NW1 3BH

10 9 8 7 6 5 4 3 2 1

ISBN   0340 69842X (PB)
0340 709359 (HB)

Printed in Hong Kong

FRANCESCA SIMON   ROSS COLLINS

Don't Wake the Baby!

Hodder
Children's
Books

A division of Hodder Headline plc

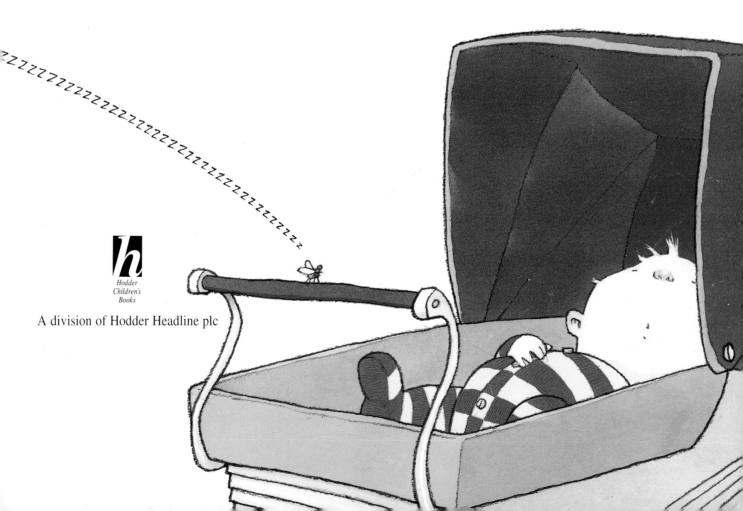

Dad was trying to get the baby to sleep.

It wasn't easy.

At last the baby fell asleep.

"Quiet everyone," said Dad. "Don't wake the baby."

A fly began to buzz round the room.
"Buzz off, fly," said Dad.
He rolled up his newspaper and...

"Gotcha!" said Dad.

Mum was making a cake, when...
ZZZZZZZZZZZZZZZZZZZZZZZZZZZZZZZZZ.

She grabbed a wooden
spoon, sneaked up
to the fly and...

THWACK!

"Quiet!" hissed Dad.
"Don't wake the baby."

zzzzzzzzzzzzzzzzzzzzzzzzzzzzzzzzzzzzzzzzzzzzzzzzzzzzzzzzzzzzzzzzzzzzzzzzzzzzzzzzzzzzzzzzzzzzzzz

Sam was eating lunch.

He sneaked up on the fly and...

"Quiet!" whispered Dad and Mum.
"Don't wake the baby."

Ellie was playing
the piano, when...

"Stop that!" bellowed Dad and Mum and Sam.

Don't wake the Baby!

They held their breath.   Everyone looked at the pram.

Aaaaaaaaaaaaaah

zzzzzzzzzz

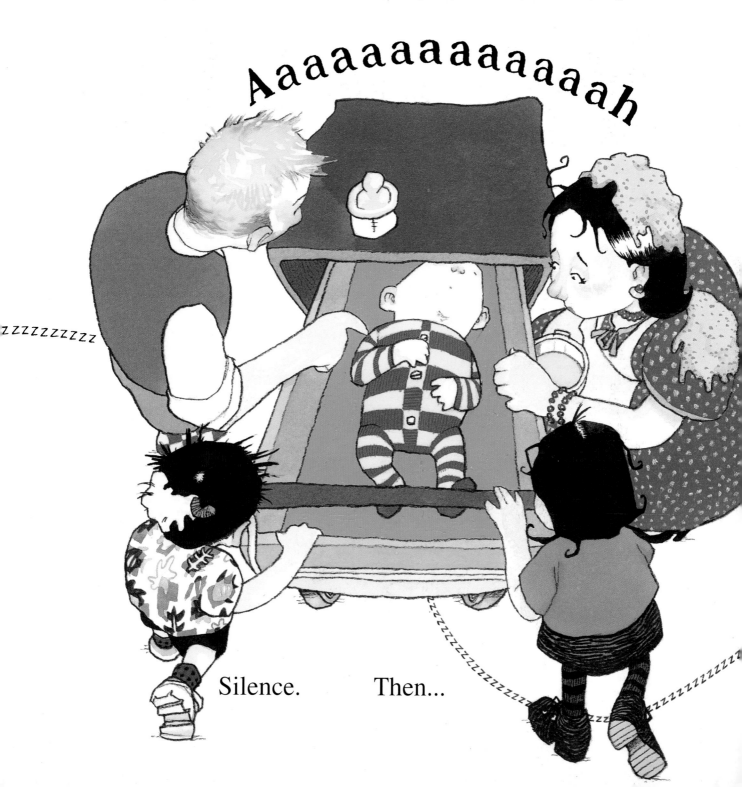

Silence.   Then...

Dad lifted his hand and...

The fly twirled
round the room.

"Dad!" they all said.
"You've woken the baby!"